STAR WARS FORCES OF DESTINY™

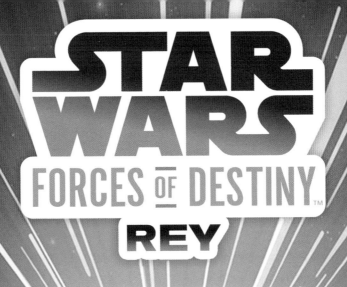

REY

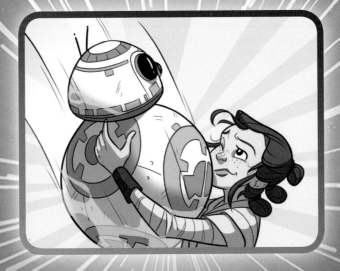

Writer
Jody Houser
Artist
Arianna Florean
Colorist
Adele Matera
Letterer
Tom B. Long
Assistant Editor
Peter Adrian Behravesh
Editors
Bobby Curnow & Denton J. Tipton

ABDO Spotlight · IDW · Disney · Lucasfilm

ABDOBOOKS.COM

Reinforced library bound edition published in 2019 by Spotlight, a division of ABDO, PO Box 398166, Minneapolis, Minnesota 55439. Spotlight produces high-quality reinforced library bound editions for schools and libraries.
Published by agreement with IDW.

Printed in the United States of America, North Mankato, Minnesota.
092018
012019

THIS BOOK CONTAINS
RECYCLED MATERIALS

Library of Congress Control Number: 2018945161

Publisher's Cataloging in Publication Data

Names: Houser, Jody, author. | Florean, Arianna ; Matera, Adele, illustrators.
Title: Rey / by Jody Houser; illustrated by Arianna Florean and Adele Matera.
Description: Minneapolis, MN : Spotlight, 2019 | Series: Star wars: Forces of destiny
Summary: On Jakku, Rey takes BB-8 home with her until someone can come for the droid, but that mission doesn't seem so easy when she has to rescue the droid from a nightwatcher worm and Teedo.
Identifiers: ISBN 9781532142956 (lib. bdg.)
Subjects: LCSH: Star Wars fiction--Juvenile fiction. | Space warfare--Juvenile fiction. | Women heroes--Juvenile fiction. | Extraterrestrial beings--Juvenile fiction. | Good and evil--Juvenile fiction.
Classification: DDC 741.5--dc23

Spotlight

A Division of ABDO
abdobooks.com

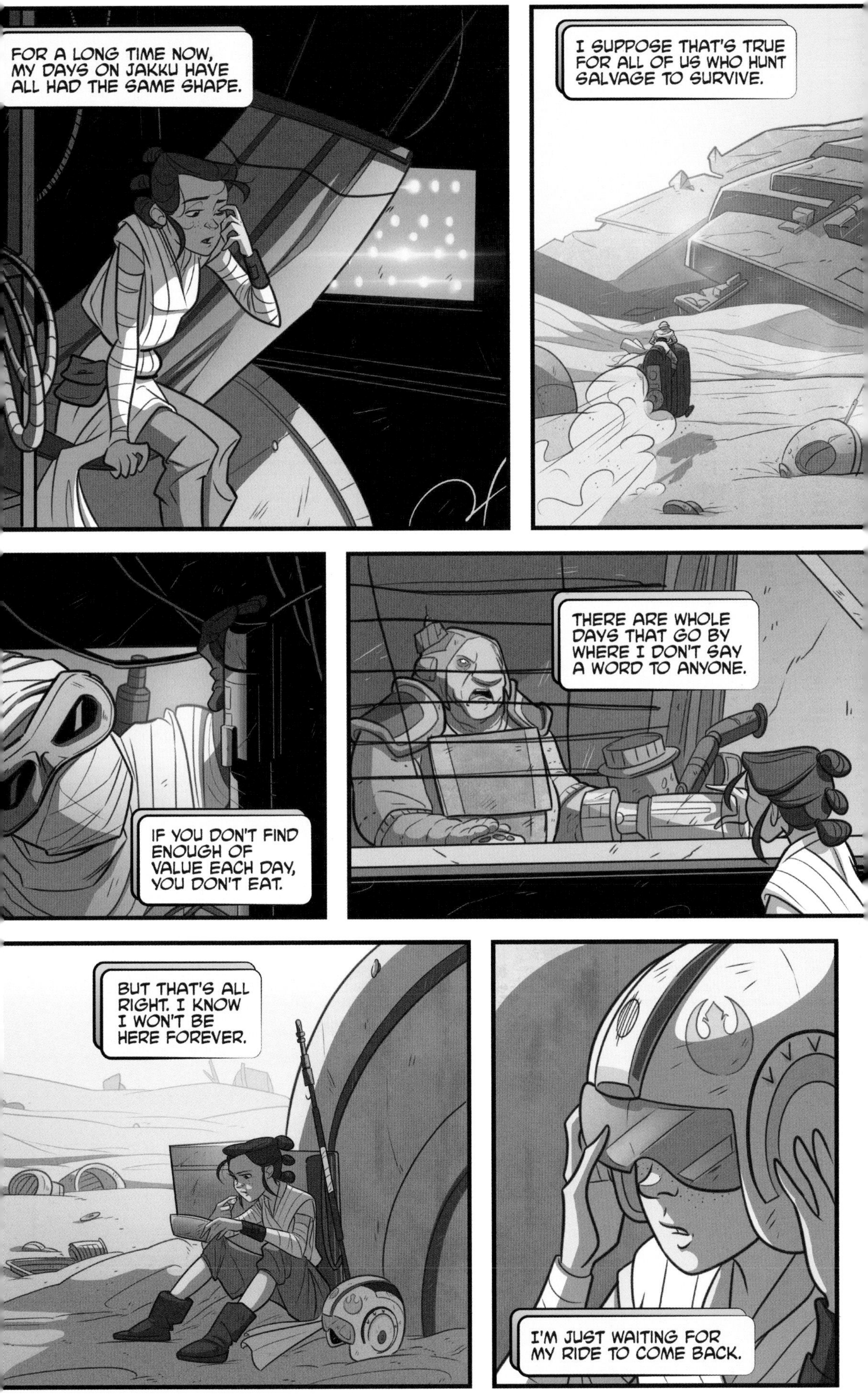
FOR A LONG TIME NOW, MY DAYS ON JAKKU HAVE ALL HAD THE SAME SHAPE.
I SUPPOSE THAT'S TRUE FOR ALL OF US WHO HUNT SALVAGE TO SURVIVE.
IF YOU DON'T FIND ENOUGH OF VALUE EACH DAY, YOU DON'T EAT.
THERE ARE WHOLE DAYS THAT GO BY WHERE I DON'T SAY A WORD TO ANYONE.
BUT THAT'S ALL RIGHT. I KNOW I WON'T BE HERE FOREVER.
I'M JUST WAITING FOR MY RIDE TO COME BACK.

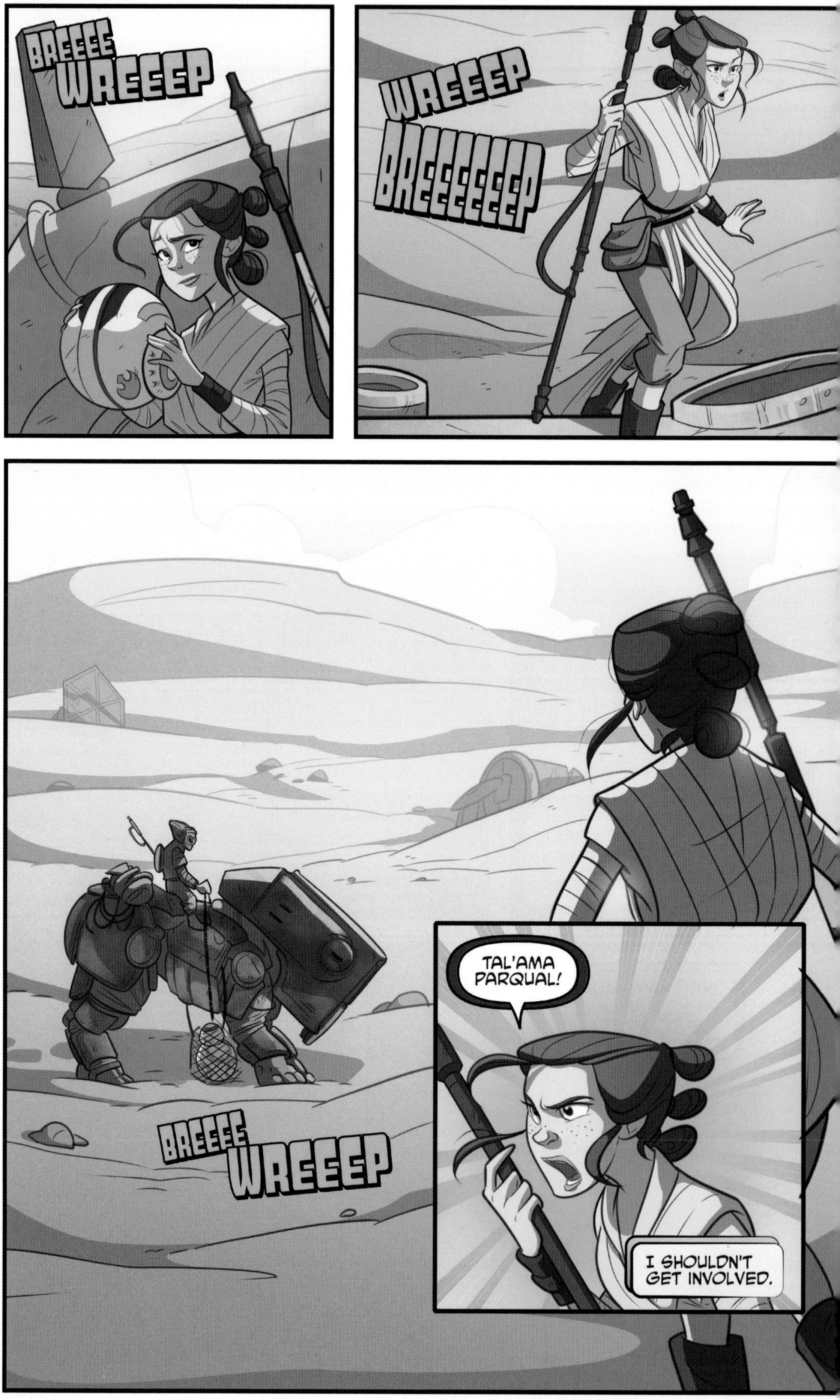

BREEEE
WREEEP
WREEEP
BREEEEEEP
BREEEE
WREEEP
TAL'AMA PARQUAL!
I SHOULDN'T GET INVOLVED.

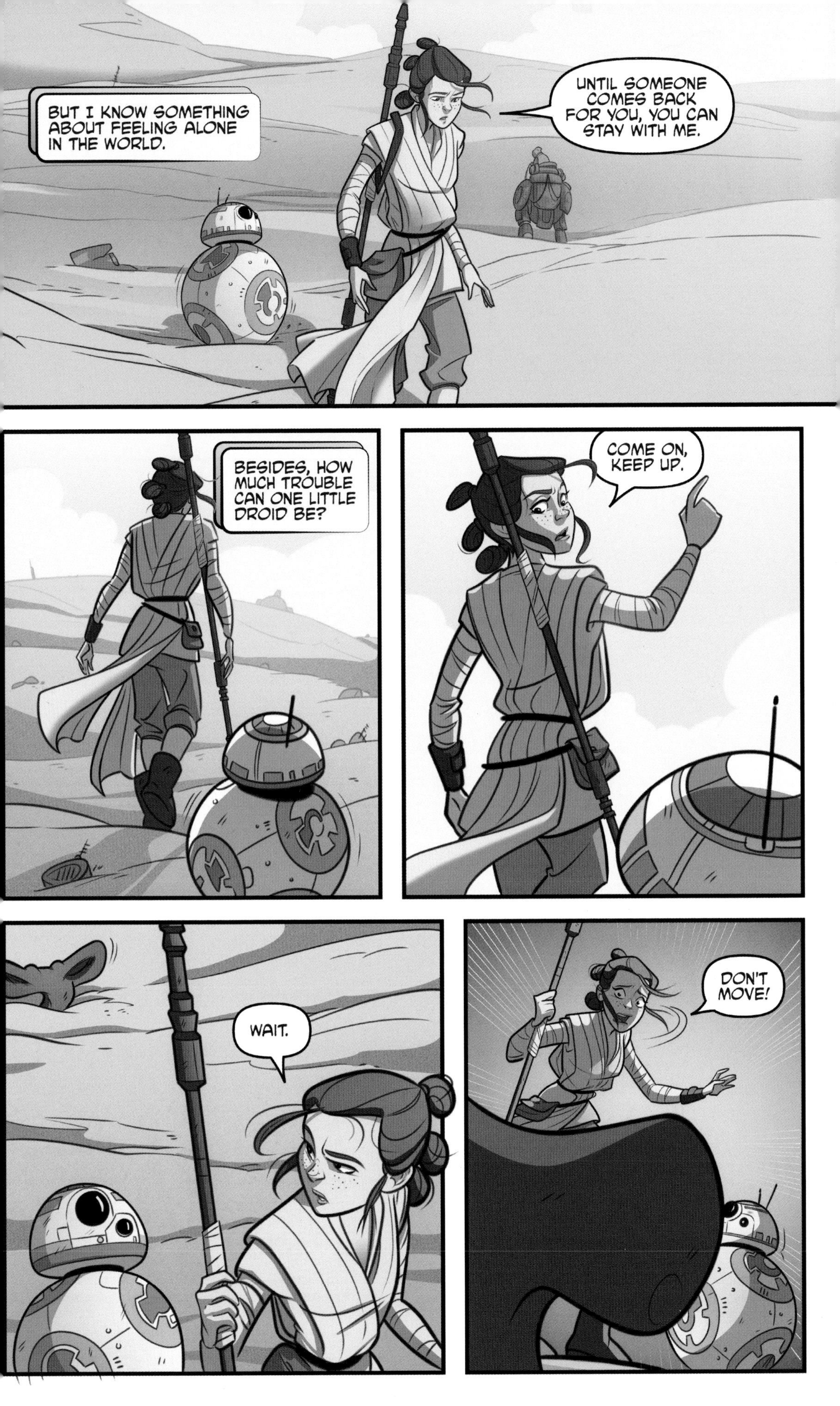
BUT I KNOW SOMETHING ABOUT FEELING ALONE IN THE WORLD.
UNTIL SOMEONE COMES BACK FOR YOU, YOU CAN STAY WITH ME.
BESIDES, HOW MUCH TROUBLE CAN ONE LITTLE DROID BE?
COME ON, KEEP UP.
WAIT.
DON'T MOVE!

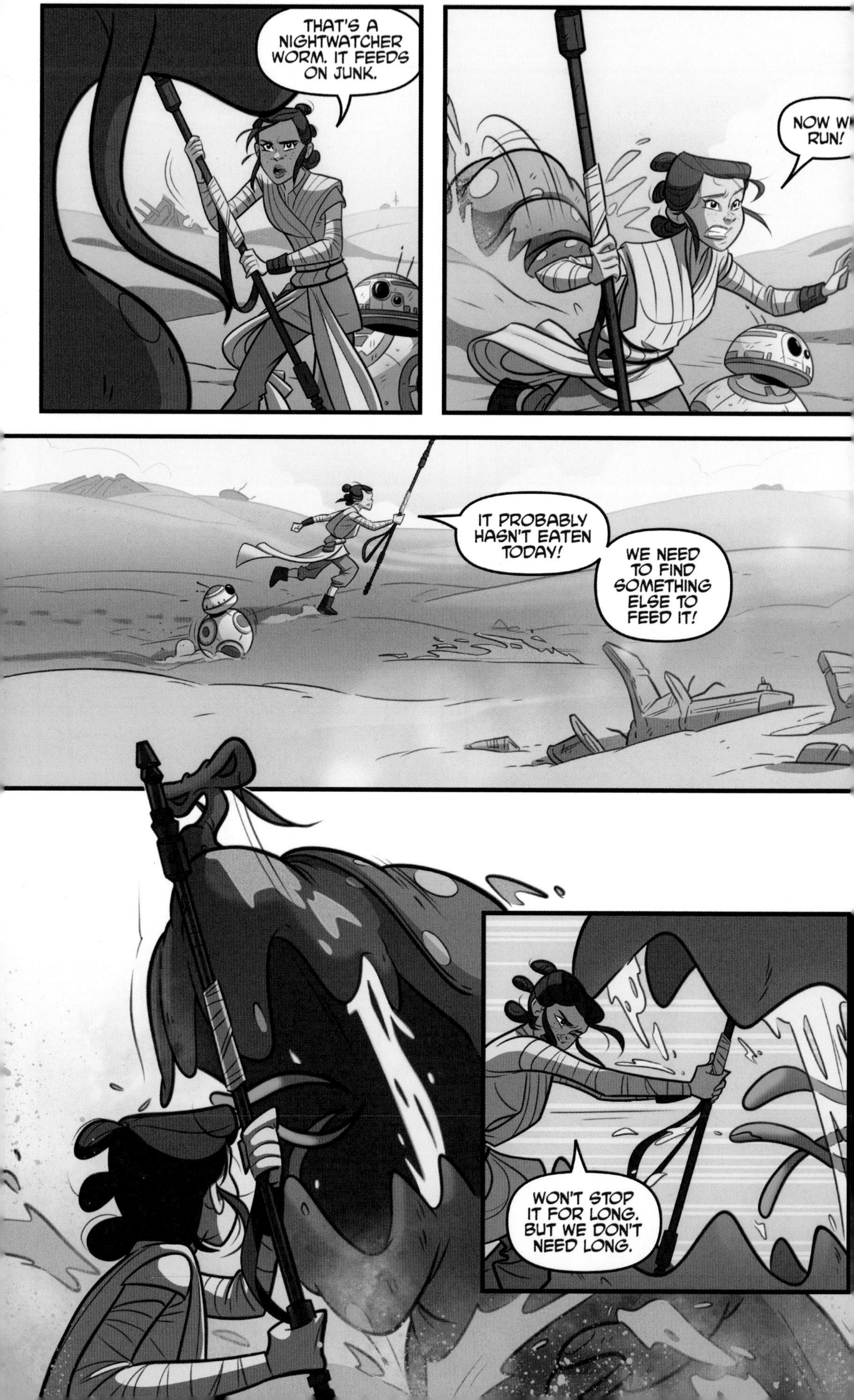
THAT'S A NIGHTWATCHER WORM. IT FEEDS ON JUNK.
NOW W RUN!
IT PROBABLY HASN'T EATEN TODAY!
WE NEED TO FIND SOMETHING ELSE TO FEED IT!
WON'T STOP IT FOR LONG. BUT WE DON'T NEED LONG.

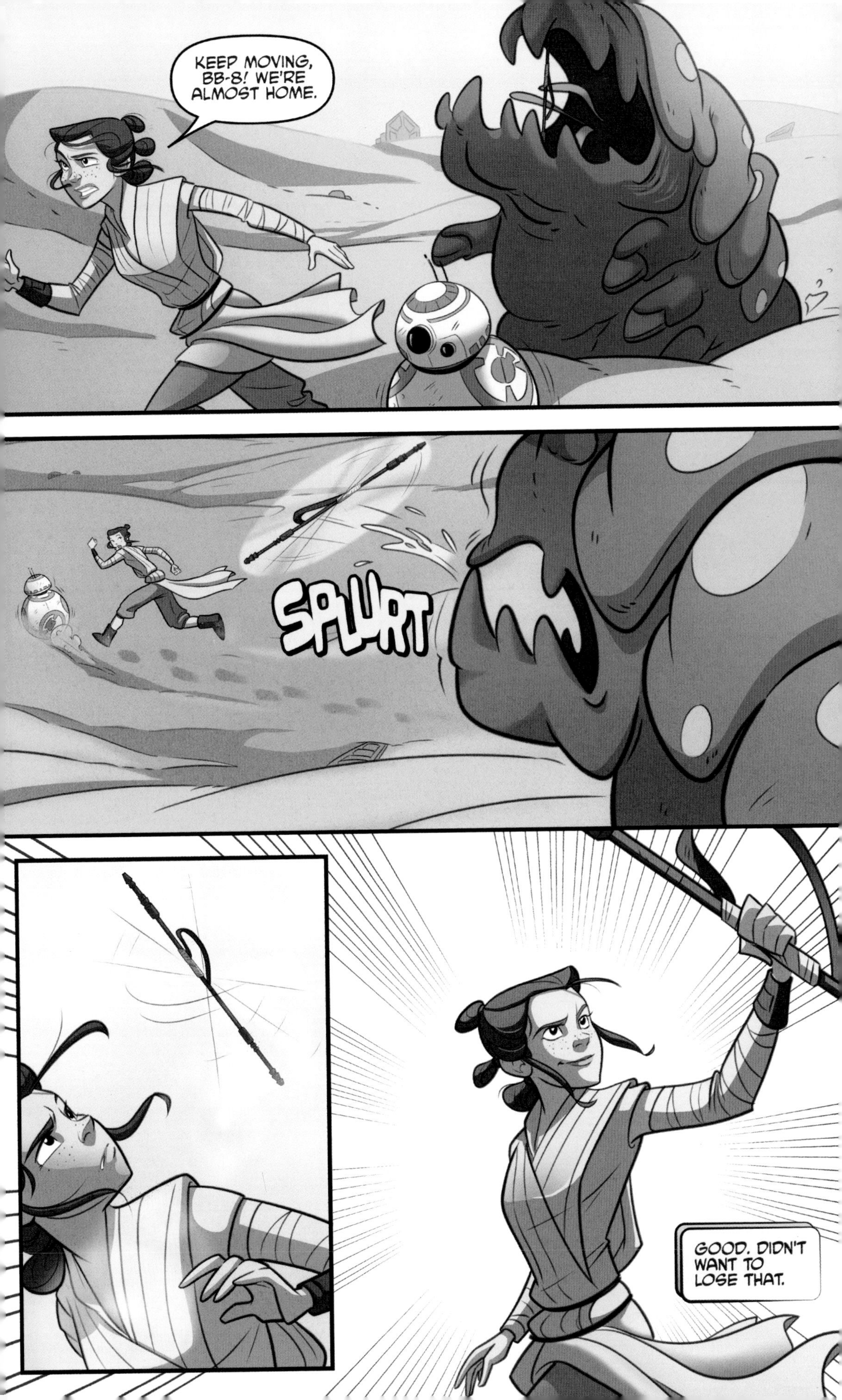
KEEP MOVING, BB-8! WE'RE ALMOST HOME.
SPLURT
GOOD. DIDN'T WANT TO LOSE THAT.

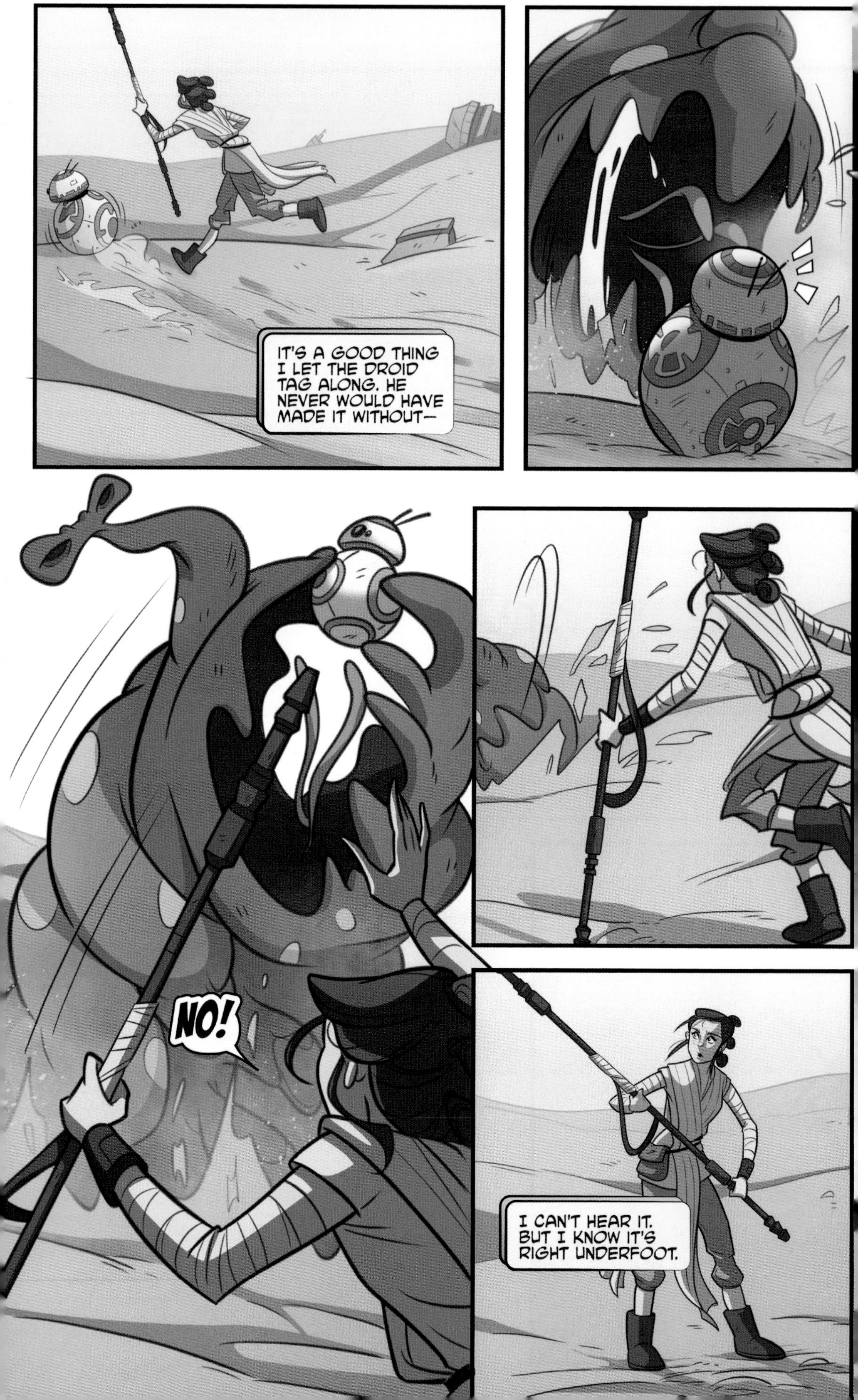
IT'S A GOOD THING I LET THE DROID TAG ALONG. HE NEVER WOULD HAVE MADE IT WITHOUT—
NO!
I CAN'T HEAR IT. BUT I KNOW IT'S RIGHT UNDERFOOT.

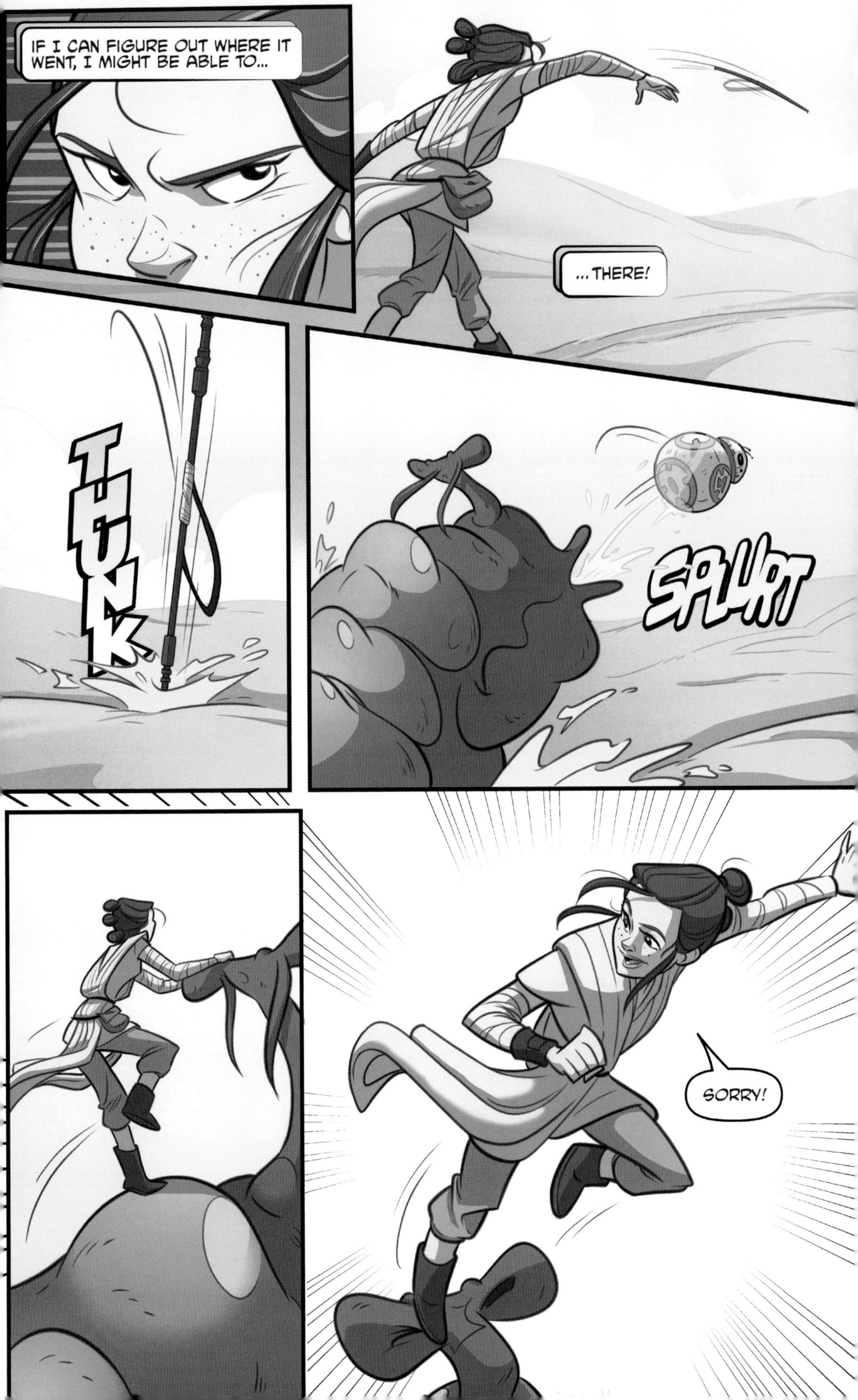
IF I CAN FIGURE OUT WHERE IT WENT, I MIGHT BE ABLE TO...
...THERE!
THUNK
SPLURT
SORRY!

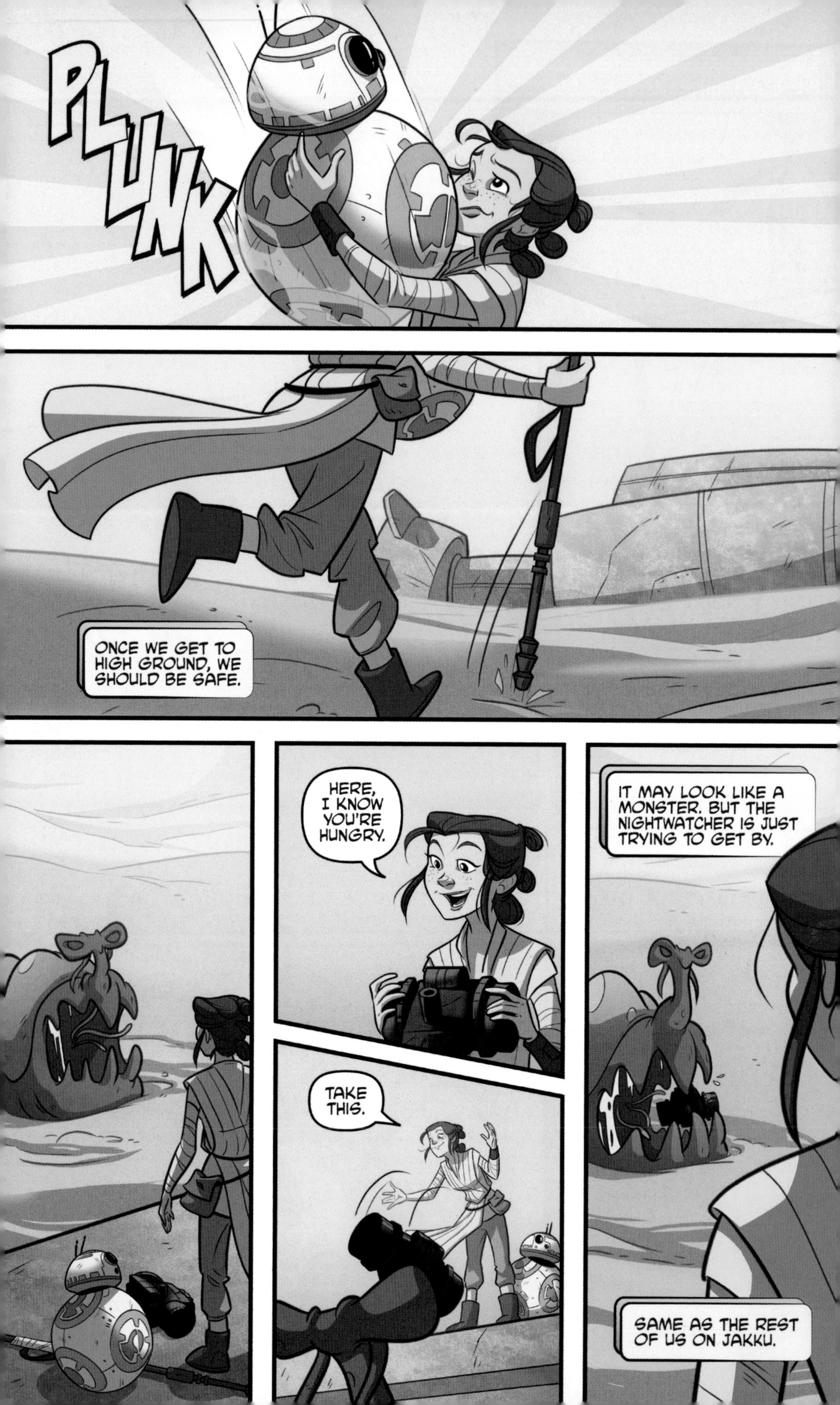
PLUNK
ONCE WE GET TO HIGH GROUND, WE SHOULD BE SAFE.
HERE, I KNOW YOU'RE HUNGRY.
TAKE THIS.
IT MAY LOOK LIKE A MONSTER. BUT THE NIGHTWATCHER IS JUST TRYING TO GET BY.
SAME AS THE REST OF US ON JAKKU.

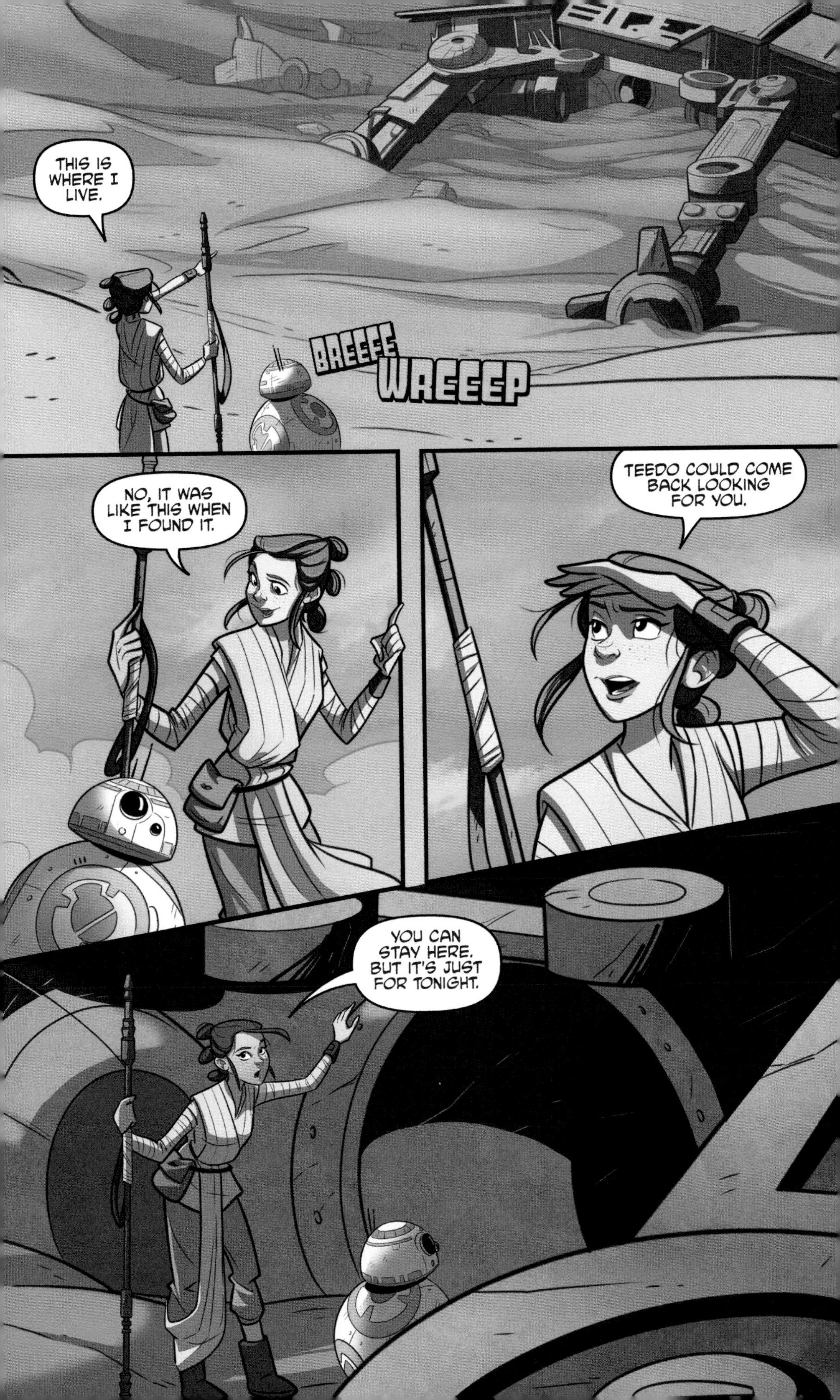
THIS IS WHERE I LIVE.
BREEEE
WREEEP
NO, IT WAS LIKE THIS WHEN I FOUND IT.
TEEDO COULD COME BACK LOOKING FOR YOU.
YOU CAN STAY HERE. BUT IT'S JUST FOR TONIGHT.

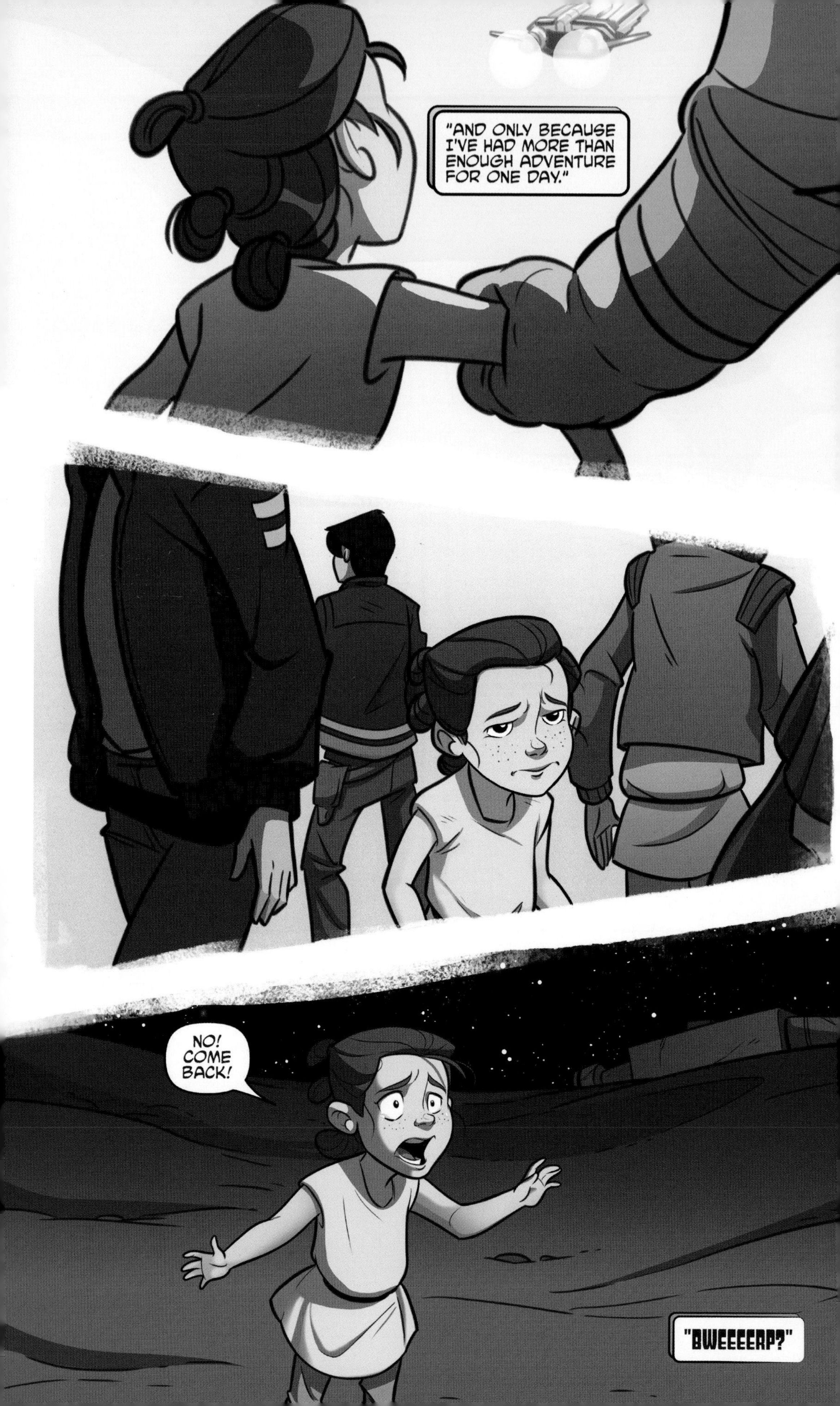
"AND ONLY BECAUSE I'VE HAD MORE THAN ENOUGH ADVENTURE FOR ONE DAY."
NO! COME BACK!
"BWEEEERP?"

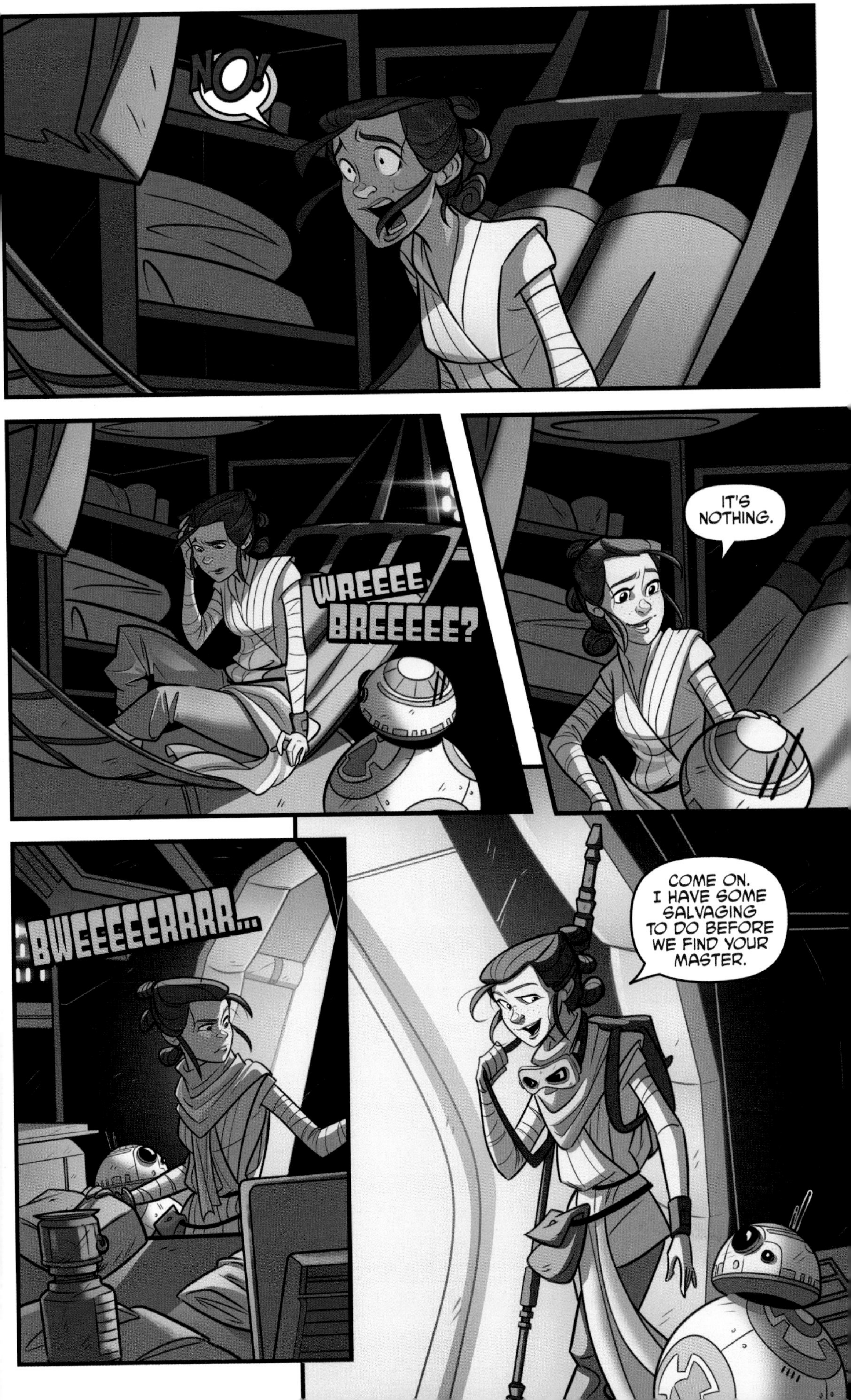
NO!
WREEEE BREEEEE?
IT'S NOTHING.
BWEEEEERRRR...
COME ON. I HAVE SOME SALVAGING TO DO BEFORE WE FIND YOUR MASTER.

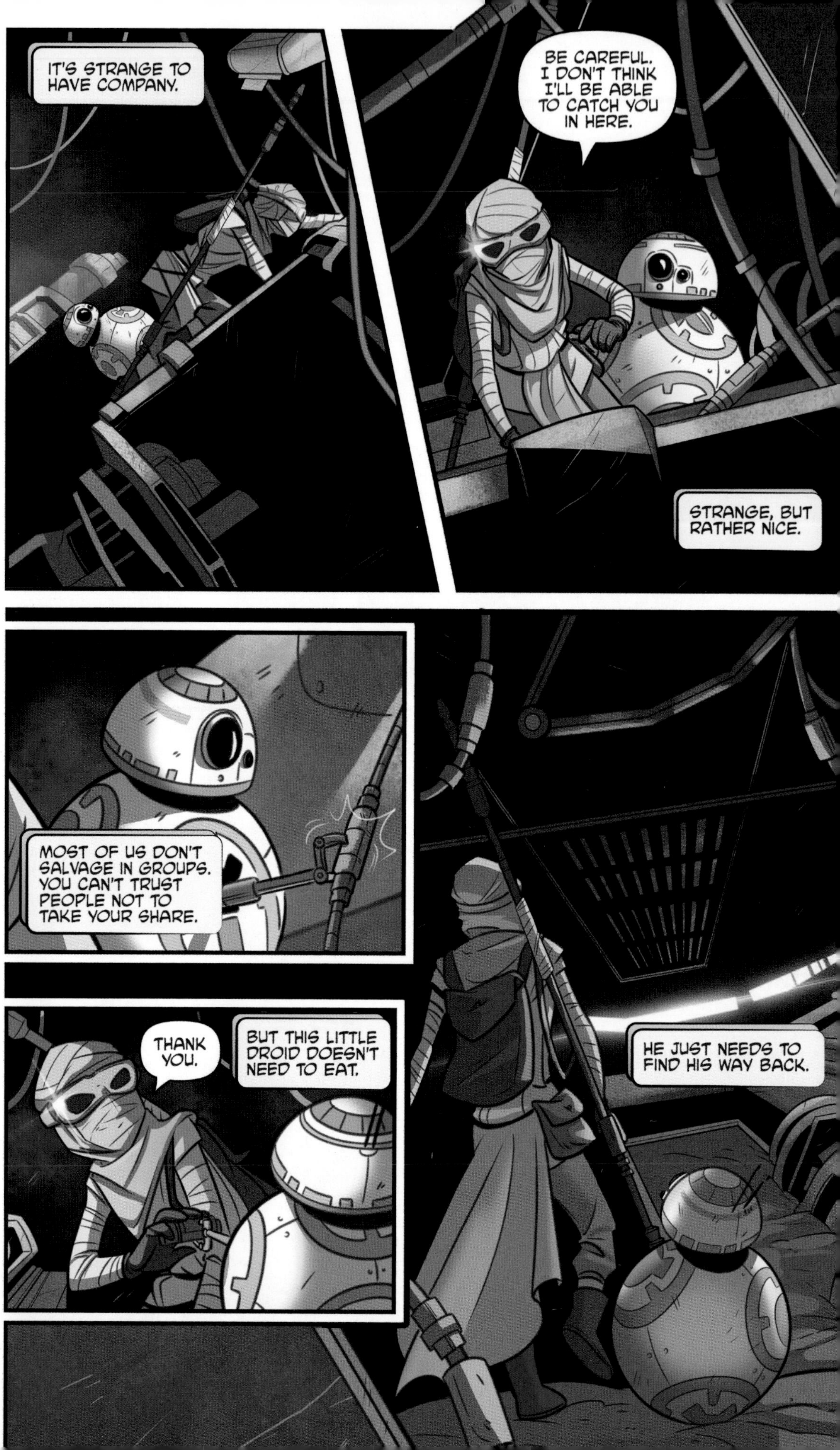
IT'S STRANGE TO HAVE COMPANY.
BE CAREFUL. I DON'T THINK I'LL BE ABLE TO CATCH YOU IN HERE.
STRANGE, BUT RATHER NICE.
MOST OF US DON'T SALVAGE IN GROUPS. YOU CAN'T TRUST PEOPLE NOT TO TAKE YOUR SHARE.
THANK YOU.
BUT THIS LITTLE DROID DOESN'T NEED TO EAT.
HE JUST NEEDS TO FIND HIS WAY BACK.

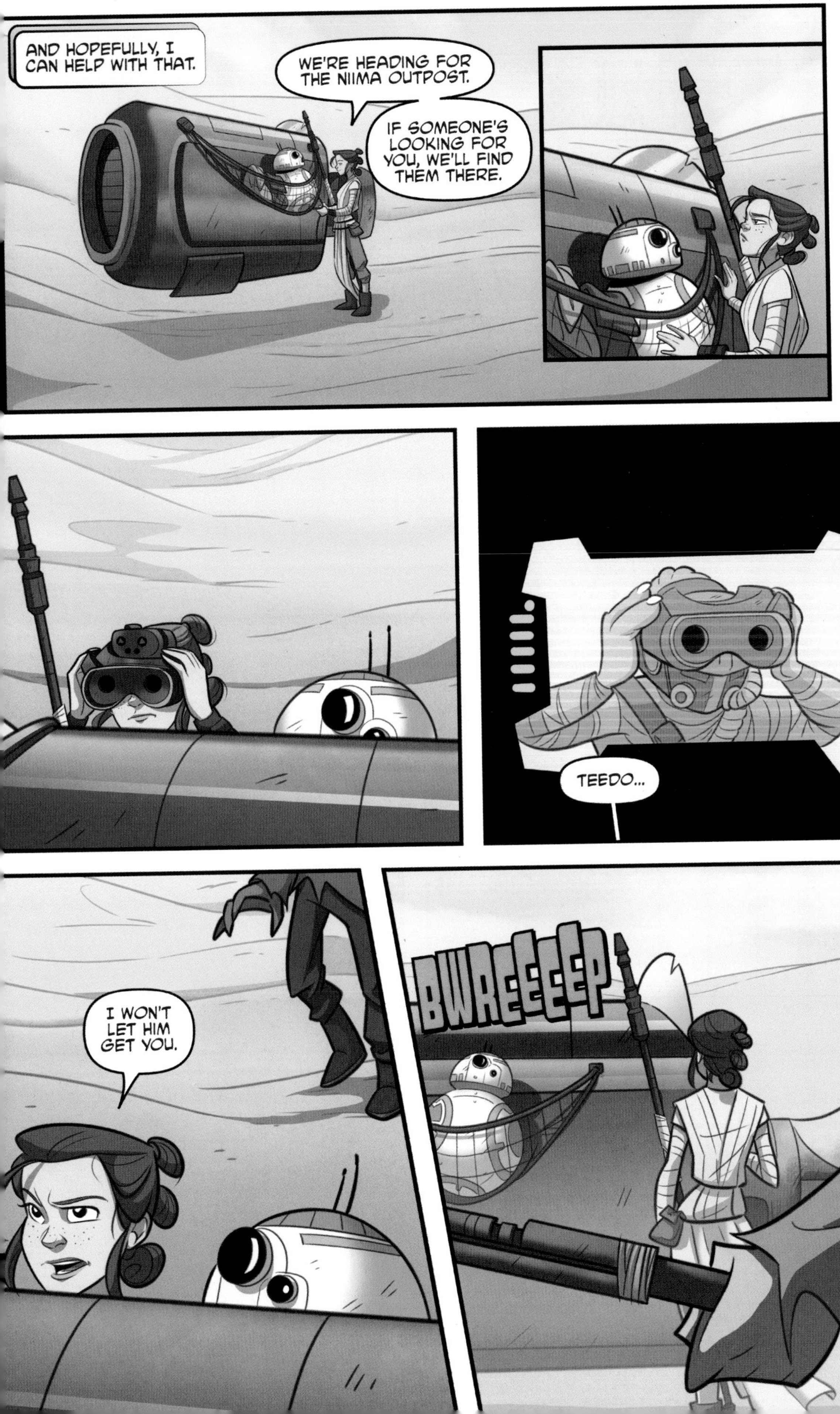
AND HOPEFULLY, I CAN HELP WITH THAT.
WE'RE HEADING FOR THE NIIMA OUTPOST.
IF SOMEONE'S LOOKING FOR YOU, WE'LL FIND THEM THERE.
TEEDO...
I WON'T LET HIM GET YOU.
BWREEEEP

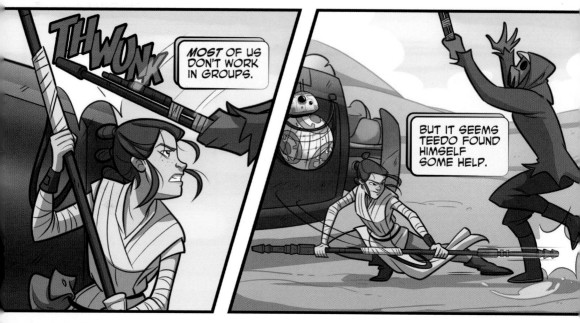

THWONK

MOST OF US DON'T WORK IN GROUPS.

BUT IT SEEMS TEEDO FOUND HIMSELF SOME HELP.

SMACK

LOTS OF HELP.

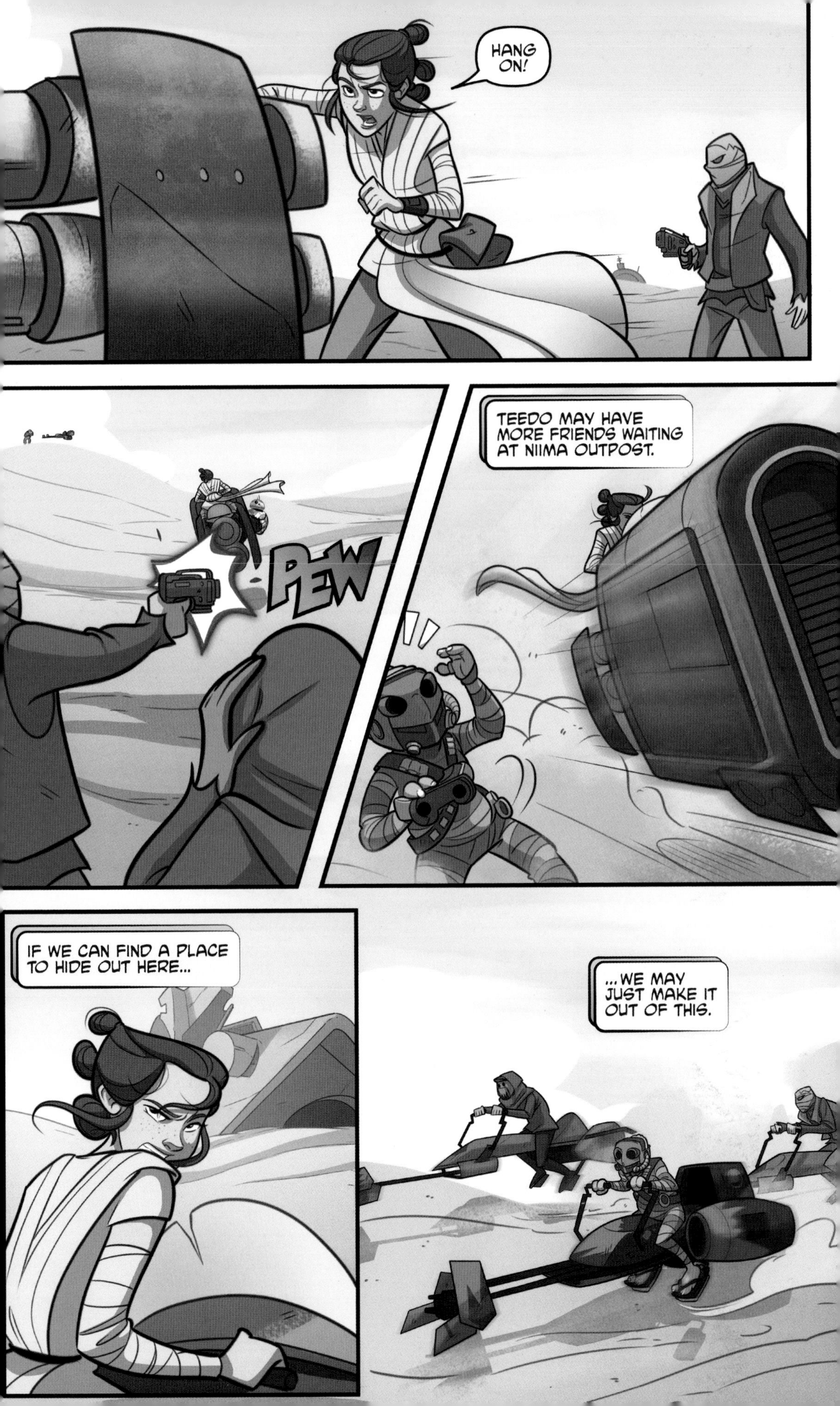
HANG ON!
PEW
TEEDO MAY HAVE MORE FRIENDS WAITING AT NIIMA OUTPOST.
IF WE CAN FIND A PLACE TO HIDE OUT HERE...
...WE MAY JUST MAKE IT OUT OF THIS.

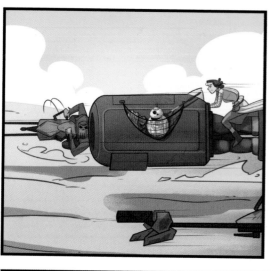

KLAAAANG

CRASH

TWO DOWN.

TURNS OUT, YOU'RE QUITE A POPULAR DROID.

WREEEP?

YES, YES! EXACTLY LIKE WITH THE NIGHTWATCHER WORM!

LET'S GO PAY HIM A VISIT...

CLEVER LITTLE DROID. HE MAY HAVE JUST SAVED US BOTH.

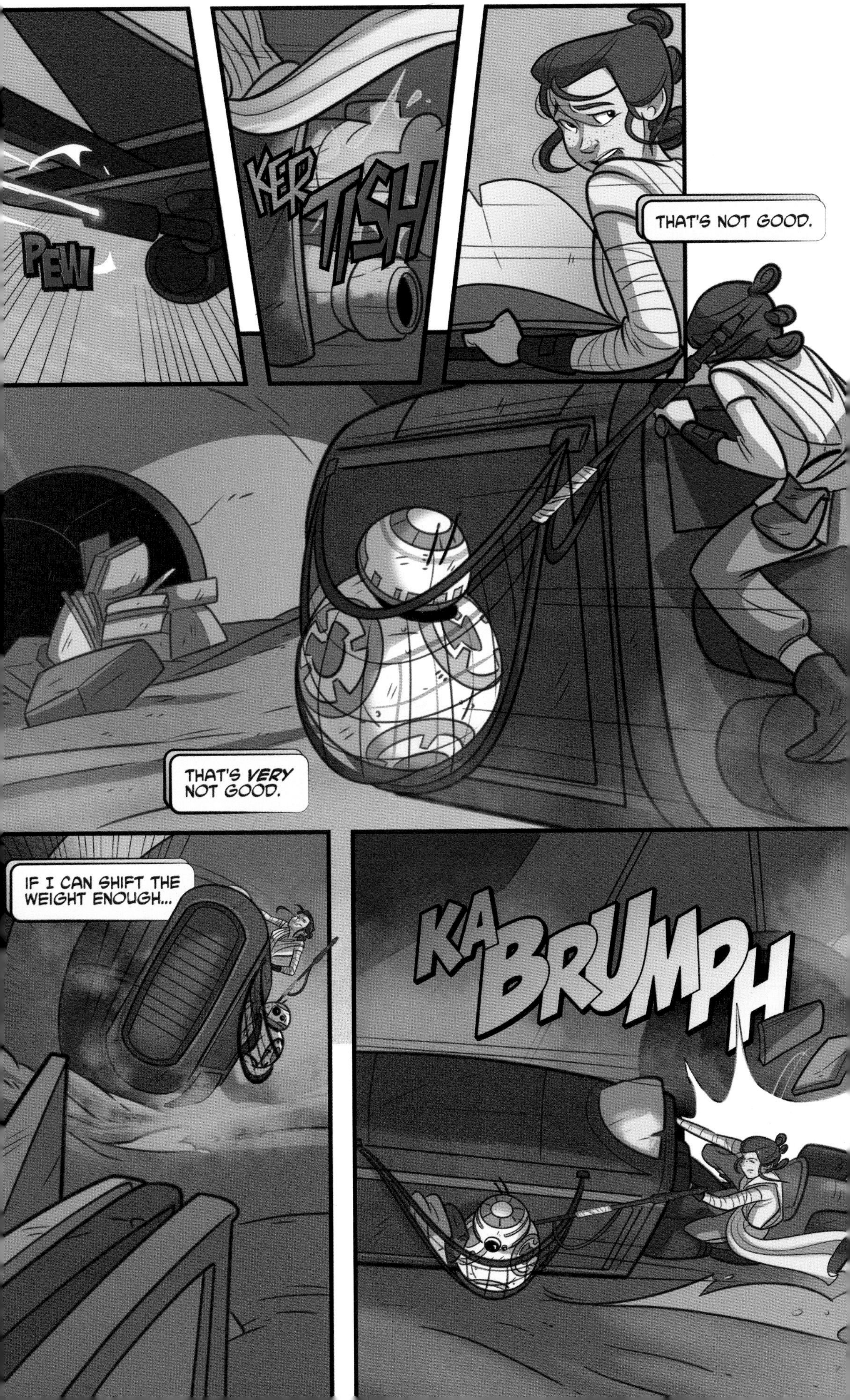
PEW
KER TISH
THAT'S NOT GOOD.
THAT'S VERY NOT GOOD.
IF I CAN SHIFT THE WEIGHT ENOUGH...
KA BRUMPH

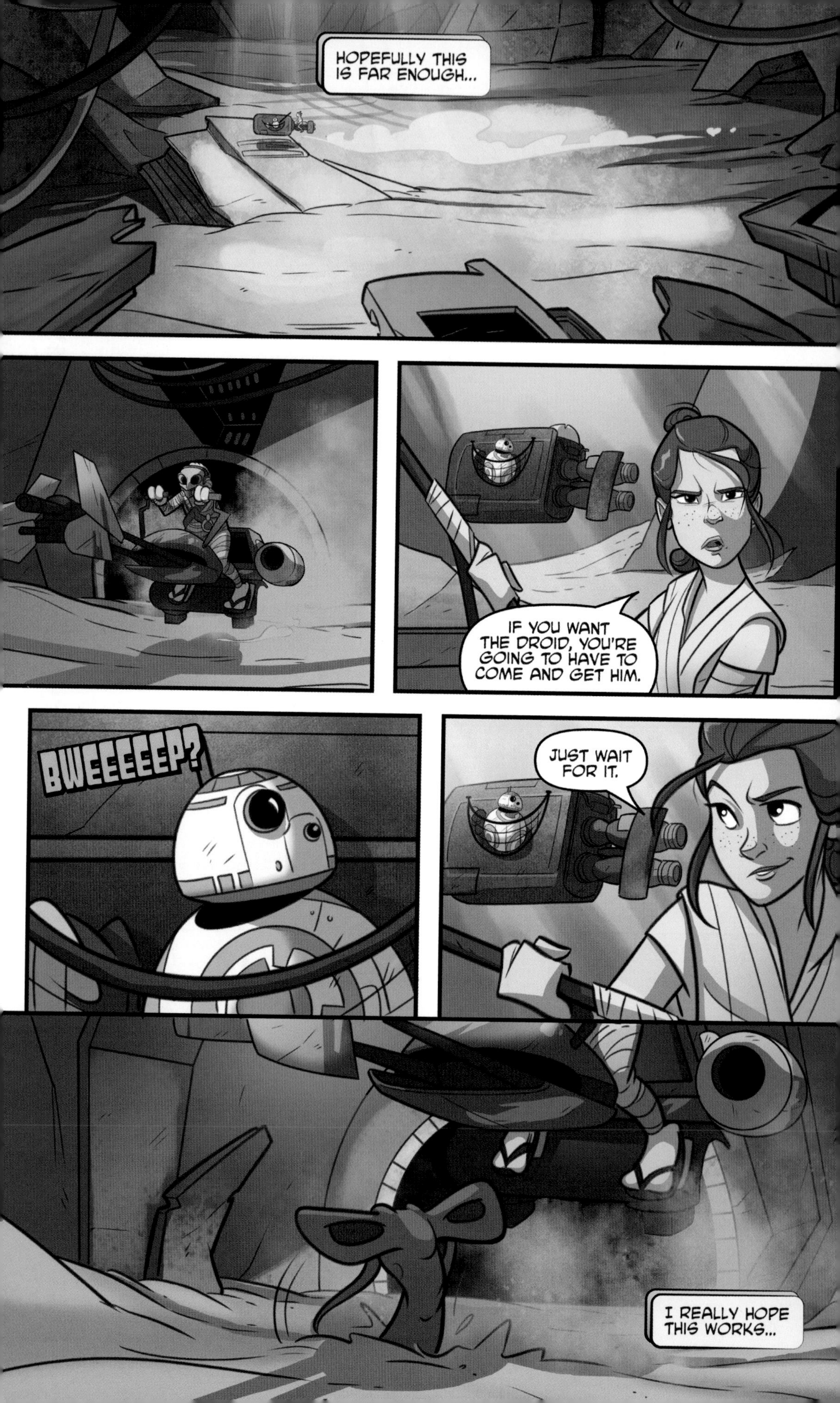
HOPEFULLY THIS IS FAR ENOUGH...
IF YOU WANT THE DROID, YOU'RE GOING TO HAVE TO COME AND GET HIM.
BWEEEEEP?
JUST WAIT FOR IT.
I REALLY HOPE THIS WORKS...

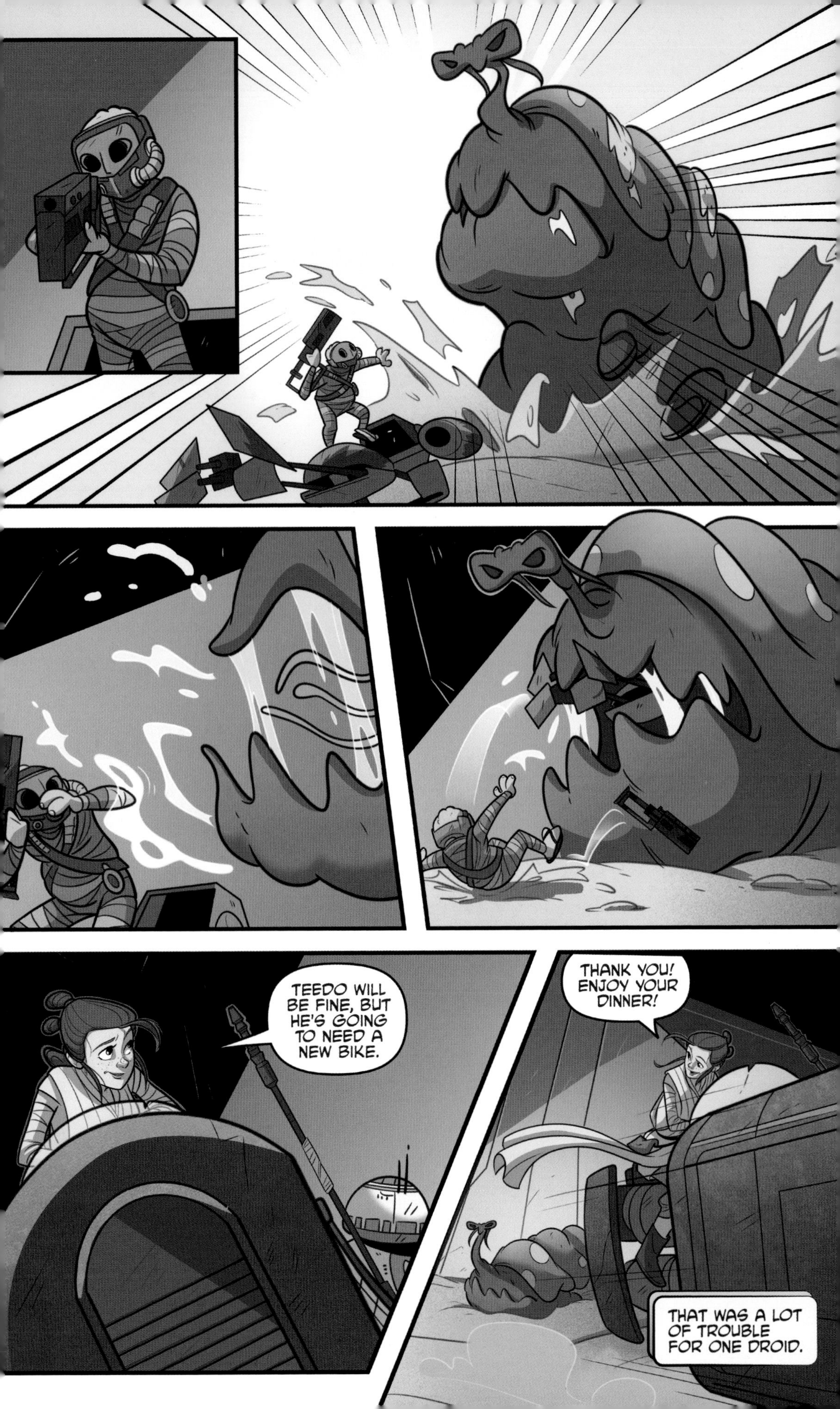
TEEDO WILL BE FINE, BUT HE'S GOING TO NEED A NEW BIKE.
THANK YOU! ENJOY YOUR DINNER!
THAT WAS A LOT OF TROUBLE FOR ONE DROID.

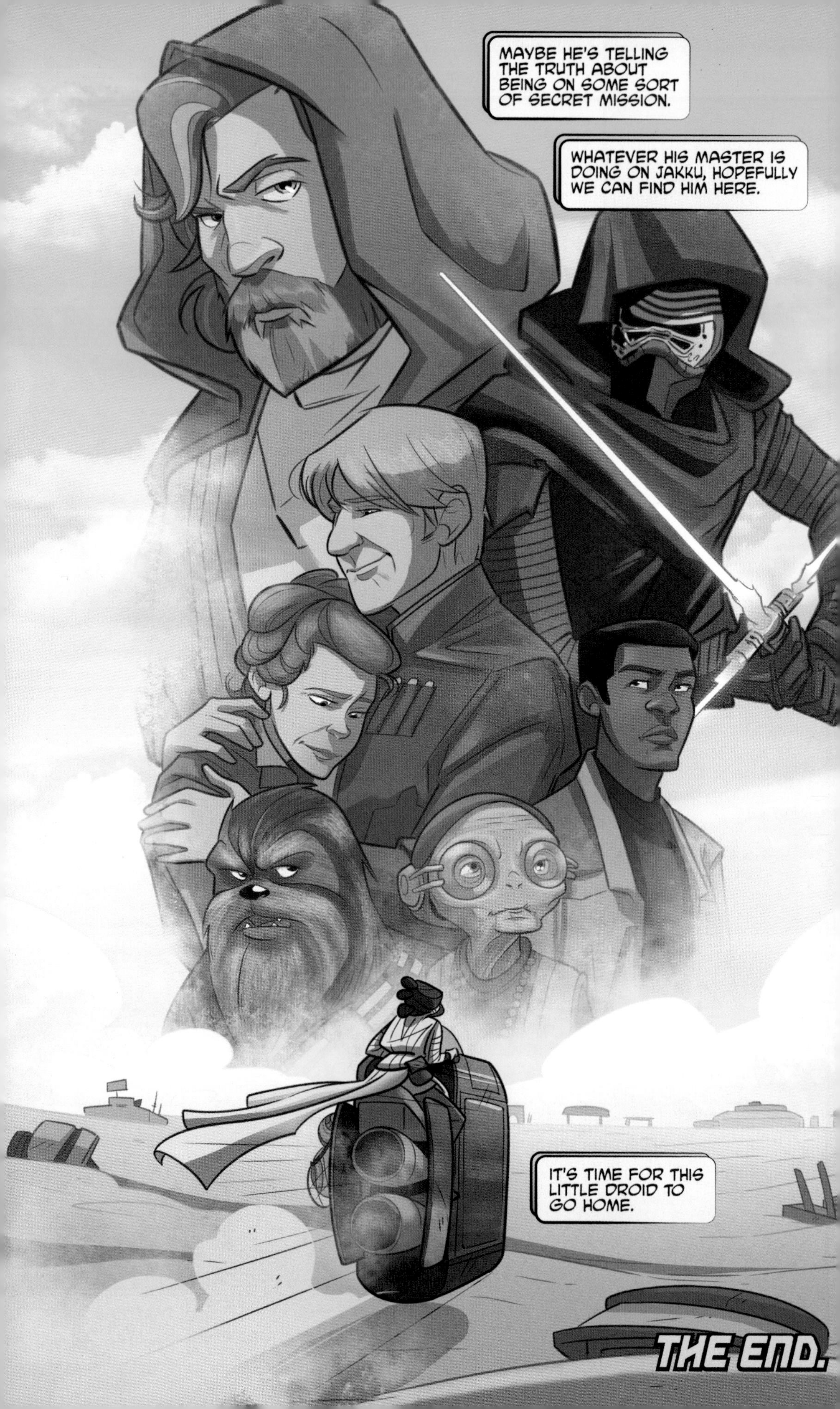
MAYBE HE'S TELLING THE TRUTH ABOUT BEING ON SOME SORT OF SECRET MISSION.
WHATEVER HIS MASTER IS DOING ON JAKKU, HOPEFULLY WE CAN FIND HIM HERE.
IT'S TIME FOR THIS LITTLE DROID TO GO HOME.
THE END.

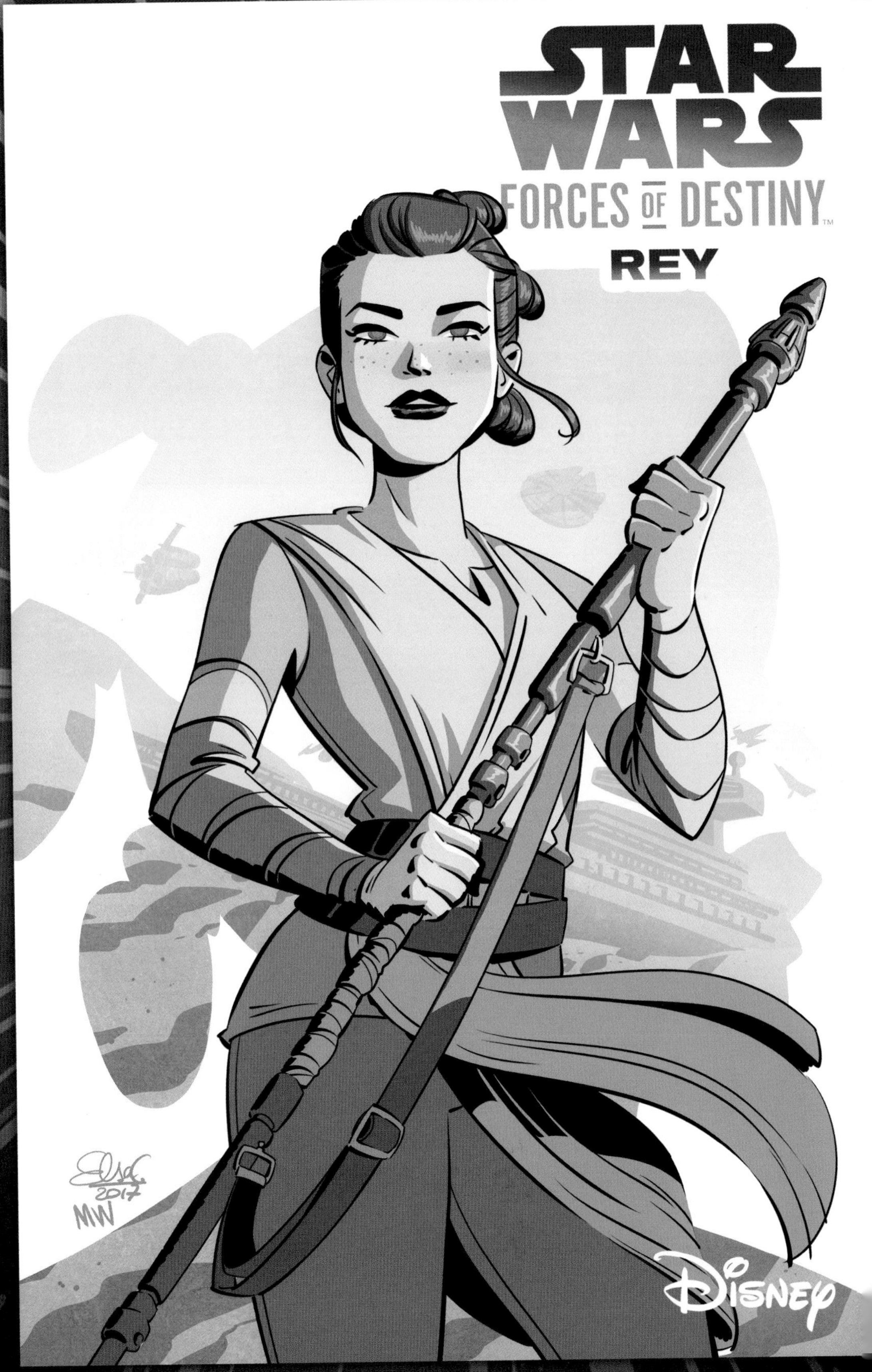
STAR WARS
FORCES OF DESTINY
REY
Elsa 2017
MW
Disney

Star Wars: Forces of Destiny "Rey"
Variant cover B artwork by Elsa Charretier, colors by Matt Wilson

STAR WARS
FORCES OF DESTINY™

LLECT THEM ALL!

Hardcover Books ISBN: 978-1-5321-4291-8

ook ISBN
-4292-5

STAR WARS
FORCES OF DESTINY
HERA

Hardcover Book ISBN
978-1-5321-4293-2

STAR WARS
FORCES OF DESTINY
LEIA

Hardcover Book ISBN
978-1-5321-4294-9

STAR WARS
FORCES OF DESTINY
REY

Hardcover Book ISBN
978-1-5321-4295-6

STAR WARS
FORCES OF DESTINY
ROSE & PAIGE

Hardcover Book ISBN
978-1-5321-4296-3